# Jaxson's Last Hour: 5:45 A.M. - 6:45 A.M.

# Jaxson's Last Hour: 5:45 A.M. - 6:45 A.M.

Tygher Williams

Order this book online at www.trafford.com
or email orders@trafford.com

Most Trafford titles are also available at major online book retailers.



Printed in the United States of America.

ISBN: 978-1-4907-1528-5 (sc)
ISBN: 978-1-4907-1529-2 (e)

*Trafford rev. 10/03/2013*

Trafford PUBLISHING® www.trafford.com

**North America & international**
toll-free: 1 888 232 4444 (USA & Canada)
fax: 812 355 4082

# Contents

# Acknowledgement

First and foremost, I thank God for giving me what was needed for me to complete this book, it has truly been a long time coming. My son, who is the Joy of my Life and I am honored to be his mother. My best friend and sister, T.M. for over 27 years, you believed in me and have always encouraged me. My editor and publishing company; for allowing my story to be read by many. I especially would like thank all of you for reading my book. As I wrote word for word, I shed many tears. I realized with each tear, I was able to walk out of the dark place that had moved into my life and had been there for over 14 years. This book is inspired by true events that have taken place in my life.

# Dedication

This book is dedicated to the memory of my baby brother, J D and my sister, M.I., you both are truly missed.

# Introduction

Death is a part of living, and surely as you are born you must die, and only God knows when your time is up and when the sands in you hour glass will run out. Dealing with the death of a loved one, friend, or family member is never easy. It seems easier to deal with death when you have time to prepare, when you know that your loved one is going to die. It gives you time to tell him or her that you love them and you can prepare to say Goodbye. When a friend, family member or loved one commits suicide it is quite difficult to deal with the fact that, that person has taken his or her life by committing suicide. It does not matter how close you were or were not to the one that has taken their life. When you get that call saying that they killed them self, there is an excruciating pain that all the morphine in the world cannot take away.

After receiving the call that my brother, Jaxson killed himself in my parents' basement, it seemed surreal, and all I wanted to hear after that was that it was a terrible and cruel joke and that my baby brother was still alive. Surely that was not the case. When your loved one kills himself or herself, you are left without closure and have so many unanswered questions.

My baby brother's untimely death was a hard pill to swallow and it left a void that will never be refilled. How do you truly deal with your life after your loved or loved ones have taken their life or lives?

# Reflection of the Two

## One

Marigold Stephanie and Jaxson both left these earthly shores during the month of March. When you lose loved ones close to your heart, you always remember what you were doing and where you were the day they passed away. The feelings that you experienced during that moment is an indescribable and numbness that no matter how many times you pray for it to go away, it just stays and it is a pain that I would not wish on my worst enemy. My loved ones died at the beginning and in the middle of the month of March.

Marigold Stephanie Brown, was the first to go on March 13, 1998. Her nick name was Gold and she was 38 years old. She was one of my older sisters. We had the same father, but different mothers. Her mother died in a car accident when Gold was about 3 years old. As a child I remembered when Gold was upset or just having a bad day, she always said, "If my mother was here I wouldn't be going through this." You see, I didn't know what it felt like to lose a mother at an early age. I am 39 years old and God has blessed me to still have my mother amongst the living. I can only imagine longing and wanting for something or someone for what seemed to be an eternity and never getting it or them. You then spend your life trying to fill that void and deep inside knowing it would never be filled.

As, I remembered Gold, she was a sister that would stand up for her brothers and sisters and she would not let anyone bother any of us. Often when a child grows up without a parent, they become an adult searching for the mother or father figure that they did not have as a child.

At an early age she found comfort in using drugs and over the years, no matter how many times, her family and friends would ask her to stop, she wouldn't. Her needs for the drugs were stronger than the need for her to stop using the drugs and the love of her family.

As, I looked back, I realized that when you have a loved one that uses drugs, the only person that they are physically hurting is themselves. Of course as a loved one it hurts you emotionally but there is nothing that you can do to stop them and the best thing to do is pray to God for their deliverance and pray to God for your sanity.

Although she was almost 14 years older than me, I didn't believe there was anything that I could have done at the time to change her mind about using drugs. I was told that she started with smoking marijuana and then it turned into full blown drug use. I believed that after many years of drug use, the drugs took a toll on Gold's body and organs. Her kidneys began to fail and she had to be on dialysis and then on March 13$^{th}$, 1998 she passed on. I believed that if she had not began using drugs, she would have still been on this side of time.

I now wondered would that be considered suicide. What else would it be called when a person puts things in their bodies for a number of years that ultimately results in their death? The only difference between someone that hangs themself, jumps off a cliff or off of a bridge, in front of a vehicle or shoots themself is that the ones that are not using drugs are they get their death out of the way immediately. Using drugs allows the individual to play Russian Roulette for many years, figuratively speaking.

When you have a relative that used drugs, you admitted to yourself that if they didn't get off of the drugs, they would eventually kill themself. You tried to mentally prepare for the day when you got that call, telling you that they had passed on.

The reality was, I just could not have prepared myself for the call that I got that day Marigold Stephanie died. I knew that I would never forget, March 13th, 1998, it was a Friday. I worked for Camp Oakland, a Juvenile Facility for Juvenile Delinquents, that were Court Ordered to be in the program as a Youth Specialist in Oxford, MI. I was at my Aunt Tina' House, I worked the 2 p.m.-10 p.m. shift. Camp Oakland was in Oxford, MI and my aunt lived in Pontiac. I stayed with my parents in Detroit, but when I worked I stayed at my aunt's house. In 1998, Pagers were used, my sister, Max kept paging me, so I called, this guy named, Micah, we were co-workers and he trained me for the job that I had. I asked him if he could call Max and ask her what the 911 was for?, my aunt didn't have long distance at that time. He called her and he called me back and told me that Gold was dead.

I was told that they took Gold to Pontiac Osteopathic Hospital. I remembered when I called and asked about my sister, the person on the other end of the phone wouldn't give me any information, even after I told her that Marigold was my sister. I mean seriously?, who in their right mind would call the hospital asking if their sister was dead? I did because a part of me couldn't believe that she was gone. I wanted someone who didn't know me or have anything against my family to tell me the truth and know that they were just doing their job. I didn't want Marigold Stephanie to suffer in death because she suffered enough emotionally and physically while she was amongst the living. Then, I realized that I was all alone and I didn't have any one to call during that time in my life.

I thought back to the last time I thought I saw her; I believed it was before Thanksgiving, November 1997. I drove down Huron Street going to Aunt Tina's House and I thought I saw Gold walking down the street. So, I circled the block so that I could talk to her; but when I made it back around the corner, she was nowhere to be found. So, I didn't really know if that was her or not.

All I knew was that I did not get the chance to say goodbye or tell her that I loved her. The sad part is I was 25 when she passed and I think the last time that I saw her face to face was when I was 14. That meant 11 years had passed since I last saw her face to face and one thing is for certain is that you cannot get time back once it has passed.

For the first time in my life, I had lost a piece of me and that piece was my sister. We had the same father, but different mothers and we were bonded by our father. I believe when you have a lot of siblings, it is definitely not all Diamonds and Pearls but it is family. We all know that everyone is going to die, as sure as they live. It is just different when it's your brother or sister. A family is like a puzzle and some puzzles are bigger than others. Before Marigold Stephanie died our puzzle consisted of a mother, a father, 4 sons and 6 daughters for a total of 12. When Marigold died a piece of the puzzle was removed permanently and with that missing piece a void was created that couldn't be refilled. So, now I had to learn to deal with that void as best as I could without grieving myself sick.

As time drew closer for the Home Going Service for Marigold Stephanie Williams-Brown, those six days leading up to the service were filled with fussing, cussing and fighting. A person would think that during the time of death in a family, that differences would have been put a side but that was not the case in our family. It was during that time that anger and hurt was voiced and that was how it was handled, as opposed to realizing that was not the time or place. It was the first time as a family that we had lost a sibling. We didn't know how to handle it nor were we taught how to deal with the death of a loved one. Previously, when a relative died, we as children, knew that someone died and that you go to the Cemetery and that is where their body stayed and the family had to deal with that loved one not being around anymore. You are not told that moving on after the loss of a loved one is a part of life.

## The Funeral

Marigold Stephanie's Home Going service was held at a Baptist church, one of her older sister's on her mother's side was a member there. The Family Hour was an hour before the actual funeral service. It was during that time I saw my father who was 71 years olds at the time break down and cried like a new born baby. I felt a gut wrenching feeling that I had never felt before, my daddy was crying and there was nothing that I could have done to stop his hurt. They brought a wheelchair in there for him because he looked like he was going to pass out. Then he was wheeled out so that he could regain his composure. I love my daddy dearly, but seeing him cry, that was not a pretty sight.

Next thing, you know, Deniece, who is our mother, was performing. It was not an Emmy Award Performance, but none the less it was a performance. She loudly said," She didn't have to go like this," as she moved side to side in a rolling motion. Now, my mother was overweight at the time, so, her belly, which looked like a big beach ball. She was moving side to side as she swung her arms and she was crying, once again, that was not a pretty sight either. As I thought to myself before real, then again, I did not know how she truly felt. What I did know was that she had been in Marigold Stephanie's life since Marigold Stephanie was 7 and she was 18. As I stood over her casket for the last time and looked at her, she appeared to have a smirk on her face. I remembered Jaxson interpreted her smile. He said that she's up in heaven saying,

"My daddy came to see me nah."

While I looked at Marigold Stephanie in her casket, I remembered, the time she stayed with us when I was about 14 and I was in the 8th grade. I came home from school and she looked at me and said, "You must have really done some work today." I asked her," why she said that?", she said, "When you do work at school you come home with your hair messed up and when you don't work at school you come home and your hair is in place." I smacked my lips and said, "Whatever", as, I thought about that conversation with Marigold Stephanie, I laughed.

During that time I remembered crying and saying, "Lord, I didn't want to burry another sibling, it was too much pain. I knew at that moment, I did not want to stand over the coffin of another sibling. I think at that moment when I was 25 I realized that death was real and that all families will have their time when they have to burry a loved one. Sure over the years I knew people that died, but it didn't really it home until it was my sister, because it had an immediate impact on me mentally.

I remembered that the choir sang so beautifully during the service. Afterwards, for that one moment, all of Marigold siblings were in one room; showing their love for her and the sad part was, she didn't get a chance to see that while she lived. There were 9 siblings, a mother and a father remaining on her father's side of the family. Marigold Stephanie, left a young adult child behind, she had done to her what had been done to her and her sister, Marsha. The difference is that her mother didn't plan to die as a result of a car accident. Gold chose to use drugs until she couldn't use them anymore.

## Two

Jaxson Matthew Williams was my baby brother and his earthly journey ended on Thursday, March 8th, 2012. Ironically, 2 days before on Tuesday, March 6th, 2012 while I was at An Effective Communication Seminar, I was thinking that March 13th, 2012 would be 14 years since Marigold passed. I then wondered which one of us would die next, not knowing, I would get the answer to that question sooner than I really wanted it. As, I was told Jaxson put his gun to his head and blew his brains out, because he believed that he had nothing worth living for and he couldn't go on. I believe that when a man or woman has a child or children that is more than reason or reasons to continue living.

Prior to this happening, my best friend, Olivia and I had a conversation over the telephone. We talked about funerals and of course because I was out of state, so, I gave her a list of the relatives that if they died, I would not attend their funeral. Jaxson was one of them because he was just Selfish as Hell and believed that the world owed him something.

I believed that his behind was too old to be thinking like that. He was grown and nobody owed him anything.

Now that he killed himself, he made a liar out of me because; I knew that I would have to go home whether I wanted to or not, because my parents had lost their son and my nieces had lost their father. This was one time where I couldn't be selfish and I needed to put somebody else's feelings before mine. As I thought back over the years growing up with Jaxson, there were good times and bad times but the good times outweighed the bad. There were certain memories that stood out when I thought about growing up with Jaxson as well as our adult lives. Even though we grew up in the same house, I couldn't remember everything about our child hood but I did remember some special moments that I will hold closer now that Jax was gone :

## Jaxson and the First Grade

I remembered that Jaxson had to repeat the first grade because he would not read when the teacher asked him too. It was not like he couldn't read. He was just that stubborn and it was apparent that the thought of repeating the first grade didn't phase him at all. So, guess what happened to Jaxson? Yep, you guessed it, he did repeat the first grade. Obviously, it truly did not bother him because he went on to the next grades after that just fine and didn't miss a beat. He was quite intelligent, maybe too intelligent for his own good. Over the years, Jaxson made it a habit to let people know just how intelligent thy were not; but none the less, that was part of who he was.

## Jaxson and Butch Wilson

Jax was not a fighter, as a child, you literally had to pin Jaxson in a corner before he would come out swinging. Then you had to call the Calvary to calm him down. During his 3$^{rd}$ grade year, he experienced being bullied by this boy named, Butch Wilson. Yes, his real name was Butch. Butch was a lot bigger that Jaxson and 90 percent of the kids in their classroom.

Jaxson was the baby boy, so needless to say, when Max got wind of the bullying by Butch, it was definitely Hell to tell the Captain. You see Butch was in the 3rd Grade, but he looked like he should have been in the 6th grade. We didn't know if he was just that big or if he had flunked several times, but nonetheless, picking on Jaxson was definitely out of the question.

I am 2 years older than Jax and Max, but Max always tried to be the boss of me. I just overlooked her because, she was harmless and there was no foul. So, quite naturally when Max got wind that Butch was picking on Jax, she did what she always did. She defended his honor because Butch was trying to besmirch his reputation. Having it said that Jaxson got bullied by Butch did not sit well with Max. Max was not a big girl, so that meant that we would be beating up Butch Wilson and there would be no questions asked.

I'll never forget that day, it was a Wednesday, and school got out at 3:15 and we all walked home the same way. We lived in the corner house off of Glendale and Wildemere and Butch lived on Sturtevant and Wildemere, which was 3 blocks away. When Max tried to plan things, she always tried to act like we were going to war, so that meant her strategy had to be in order and we had to be ready when it was time to put **Operation Get Butch** into play.

## ⌛ Operation get Butch

The time had finally come and Maxine put Operation get Butch into place. Jaxson and I were briefed on the part that we would play in Maxine's Strategic Plan. Since we all stayed off the corner of Wildemere. Maxine decided that we would walk down Lawton to go home. She chose that street because Jax and Butch were dismissed from the door closest to Lawton.

Jaxson told Butch that they would be fighting after school on the corner of Lawton and Leslie, Butch had no idea what was in store for him. The time had come, I could only imagine that Jaxson was shaking in his shoes like rat turds in a chestier drawer. You had to understand that Jaxson normally would not initiate a fight, but he wouldn't run from one either. It was so funny because both of the boys had their cheering section. I stayed in the background, but for the life of me, I couldn't figure out where Max was, but I knew she would show up when it was time like Bobby Mercer in "Four Brothers".

They finally got to the spot and Jaxson just stopped and while Butch talked Jaxson stepped back and came full force with a Round House Punch, we all were caught off guard. Butch hit the ground and one of his friends said, "You got the snot knocked out of you". Butch tried to get up, but before anything else could be said, Maxine came from out of nowhere full force and kicked him straight up his crack. So much for her Strategic Plan I didn't see any need for me to jump in, the twins handled it without their big sis and their bond grew stronger. Needless to say after that Butch didn't bother Jax anymore. In fact Butch tried to become Jax's friend, but Max told him, that they both had a mutual understanding and that was good enough.

## ⌛ Jaxson Becoming a father at 17

Growing up Jaxson, was tied to Momma's Apron String, so you can imagine what I was thinking when he told us he was going to be a father. As far as I knew he was still a virgin, boy was I wrong, because he became a father at the age of 17. Jaxson got his first Girlfriend in the 10th grade and prior to that any girl that he mentioned he like, was a **No Go.** He was the youngest boy in the family and no female was good enough for him. Jaxson was in the band for his 9th and 10th grade year. Well that was the place that none of his siblings were and that was where he met Crystal and their relationship developed. During the Spring Semester of his 10th grade year, he began coming home late and we never thought anything about it.

Afterwards, we found out that he spent that time walking Crystal home and getting to know her family, while his family was none the wiser. Yes, I had always been an Investigator, but this was one time that my investigation skills failed me horribly. Little did we know that those 2 had gone half on a baby. Almost 6 months after turning 17 he became a father. It was during that time I realized that my baby brother, had grown up to a certain degree and right before my very own eyes and I hadn't paid it any attention.

After becoming a Teenage Dad, you could see that Jaxson had changed from a boy to a man. Granted he had to become an adult before his time due to having a child, but he followed through with that responsibility. He finished school and worked while he did it, played football, maintained his GPA and never lost focus on the reason why. It just seemed like becoming a teenage father, changed his perspective on life. Jax completed his high school career by going to his prom.

## ⌛ Jaxson's Prom and Graduation

The time had come for Jaxson's Prom and of course, he took Crystal. It made sense because she took him to hers', they were still a couple and they had a child together. He wore Green and Black and he rented a Limo. I guess neither one of them wanted to be responsible for driving. All I knew is that evening, Jaxson was clean and too hot to touch for his prom. You could see the joy and happiness on his face.

Jaxson going to the Prom was a Rite of Passage. He was one step closer to walking across that stage so that he could graduate from high school and this was his last activity as a High School Student. He had grown up right before my eyes and he had not become a statistic in the African American Community and that was truly something to be proud of. His graduation had come and afterwards the family went out to dinner to celebrate. While at the table, we all demanded that he give a speech.

## ⌛ Jaxson's Speech

Jaxson stood up and gave his speech. He informed us that during the second semester of his twelfth grade year that he missed an entire month of school, contemplating what he was going to do with his life. He told us that he did not plan on becoming a father before he had a wife, but he would not change it for the world because Crystal and Jackie was his everything.

He said that becoming a father at 1, changed his whole perspective. He now had someone that was depending on him and someone that he could love unconditionally. Jax said, "When he looked in his daughters eyes, he saw nothing but love and innocence". Jaxson made it very clear that being selfish was no longer an option. He had to step up to the plate and embrace his manhood and responsibility. The responsibility of being a father as well as being a man, play time for him was now over.

He said, "He knew that he was going to make mistakes, get bumped and bruised. He asked us as his family to continue to love him and pray for him no matter what and most of all if there was anything to be said about him, to say it to his face". He reminded us that in the event that we wanted to point our finger at him, that we had at least 3 fingers pointing back at us. None of us were prepared for the speech that Jaxson gave, but it definitely brought tears to our eyes and gave us something to think about.

## ⌛ Jaxson and Alabama State University

Jaxson got a partial Football Scholarship to Alabama State University. During that time I was already attending ASU. I decided to sit out Fall 1994, so that I could work and earn enough money to get a car and that is exactly what I did. While I worked to get my car, Jaxson was supposed to be there one semester without me.Then, I would return to school Spring 2005 and we would have a car to get around Montgomery, AL. I just knew that he would be okay, but I was sadly mistaken. He left on a Saturday going to attend General Orientation and then begin his College Life as a Football Player.

Needless to say, by the next Thursday, he was calling and crying to come home. Jaxson had never been outside of Detroit until he left going to Montgomery. I remembered my first week there; I called crying to momma telling her that I wanted to come home and she told me that there was nothing in Detroit for me and I needed to stay my behind in Montgomery. I did just that, during that time I felt like my mother didn't want to continue to have to feed another mouth. So, I stayed and graduated with a Bachelors of Science Degree in Criminal that I received from Alabama State University, an Historically Black College and University in August 1997. My mother didn't want me back home, so, I was determined to get that degree and make something of myself.

Things were different with Jaxson, after all he was the youngest boy in the family and Marsha and her husband paid for Jaxson's Plane ticket to come back to Detroit. Once he returned home, he said that he missed Crystal and Jackie and he let my mother know that she was going to be a grandmother again. He also told us that he couldn't deal with those girls that were trying to climb through his room window because he played football.

After it was said and done, Deniece made it very clear that she blamed Mat for Jaxson not staying and completing his College Degree. She made it known that if Matthew had taken us on Family Vacations while we were growing up, then Jaxson would have been use to leaving the state.

I was disappointed in Jaxson when he returned from ASU, I believed in my heart that he didn't give it a chance. I shared that with him and he told me that college is not for everybody and nobody knew what he was feeling, because none of us became a parent at the age of 17. He said that alone made his journey more difficult than ours. He said no one knew how it felt to be a parent and know that you couldn't take care of yourself, so how are you supposed to take care of a baby, when you are still a baby yourself. The tears in his eyes at the moment made me realize that my baby brother was more terrified than I could have ever imagined.

I felt horrible inside because I didn't think about how he felt or what he was going through. I knew the thought of me having a baby before I got grown was something that I didn't want to experience. I realized at that moment, that I would never walk in Jaxson's shoes, so I would never truly know how he felt. I told myself at that point, I would help him when he needed me.

## ⌛ Jaxson Married

Jaxson and Crystal were still together they now had 2 daughters and a 3rd one on the way. They both decided it was time for them to get married and become husband and wife. Jaxson made it very clear that he remembered as a young boy being told that marriage is honorable in God's Eye Sight and shacking would send them to hell quickly in a pair of Gasoline Drawers on a ski slope.

Jaxon vowed on his life that he would be a husband to Crystal, a father to his daughters and the provider that his family needed. They got married in June 1996, Jaxson took his new responsibilities very serious, he left his mother and father and clung to Crystal, his wife.

While we were growing up, we all promised each other that we would be better parents to our children then our parents had been to us. We would use the examples that our parents set and be the opposite to our children. There were many days that our lights, water and gas were off. Not to mention the countless nights that we went to bed hungry, because Mat and Deniece would spend their money playing the lottery, because their gambling addiction meant more to them than the well-fare of their children. As long as Jaxson was married, he kept his distance from us because he didn't want to be reminded of the traumatic childhood that he experienced.

He fell in love with Crystal because she accepted him for him and she taught him to love himself and she willingly accepted the love that he had to offer. Jaxson experienced love and learned what was required of a parent and proudly kept his married life between himself and his wife.

Those two were in love with each other and they did not let their families interfere. They handled their household and relationship between the two of them. As far as the family knew, they had the perfect marriage with its ups and downs.

## Jaxson asked for a Little Help

During that time Jaxson asked for a little help, he and Crystal were back together trying to work it out for the sake of their daughters, but he wasn't stepping up to the plate. So, one day we had a conversation. I asked him what was wrong and he told me that he just needed a little help getting a better job. Well at that time, I was a Case Manager for a Work First Program in Detroit. So, one of the things that we helped our clients with was training. I contacted one of our training partners and let him know that I had a brother that needed some training so that he could get a better paying job and provide for his family.

He told me what to tell Jaxson and when Jaxson needed to report for training. Jaxson understood that a favor was being done, so that he could do what he needed to do for his family. Jaxson was provided with the opportunity and received a hand up. As a result of that training Jaxson was able to maintain steady employment and provide for his family. I didn't mind helping him because he was my brother and somebody helped me, when I needed help. Because of the help that I received I was able to help others as well. Being able to put my brother in contact with someone that could open more doors for him, made me proud and I felt like a big sister helping her baby brother. The job that Jaxson had at the time of his death was a result of the help the he received based on a phone call that I made because at the time, I knew someone who had the ability to help my brother beyond my capability.

## Jaxson Divorced

Jaxson was so in love with Crystal and we were all shocked, when she called Deniece and told her that she needed to come and get him. Deniece and Max headed to Crystal and Jaxson's house to see what the problem was. By the time they got there Jaxson had ripped the side of Crystal's t-shirt out of anger, he walked in and found another man in their house. Come to find out Crystal got caught cheating on Jaxson, not once but So, he did what any man would have done. He put those hands in that man's life and from that point on Jaxson had done 180 degree turn.

Prior to getting caught cheating none of Jaxson's Family was in their business because they kept their marital business to themselves. Crystal made the mistake that a lot of people make in their relationship, she invited the in-laws in and we all know once the in-laws are in they don't leave willingly, they have to be put out with love. It was not until after Crystal got caught cheating that we all realized just how hard Jaxson loved.

At that point Crystal realized that she should've messed with a Bear in a pair of Gasoline Drawers on fire than getting caught cheating. We all realized that Jaxson loved her more and somewhere along their journey as husband and wife, she stopped loving him enough to keep her legs closed to other men.

He went from being a loving husband and father to being a person that wanted to make her hurt the way that she had made him hurt. Jaxson knew that no woman wanted a male in her house that was not providing for his household. His mindset was that 2 could play that game Crystal chose to play. So both of them played and the sad part was their daughters suffered as a result of the choices that they both made. Jaxson who once tried to be the example of what a husband, father and provider should be; then became the typical deadbeat and that was who he chose to become.

After Crystal had enough she put Jaxson out, he moved back in with our parents and the icing on the cake was that he got served with Divorce Papers on May 19th, 2003, which happened to be his 28th birthday. He said, "Happy F* * *g Birthday to me".

It appeared that after his divorce was finalized he became a Lover of all the ladies. The anger and hurt that Jaxson felt for Crystal he then directed towards all the other women that he dated. I told him that he had sisters and daughters and the way that he was treating the women that he was dealing with would come back on all of us. He responded, "There is Collateral Damage in every war". I realized then that we were the Collateral Damage of their war". I told him that, "Nobody, not man or woman deserved to be treated the way that he was treating those women, and that he would most certainly reap the seeds that he sowed".

## ⌛ Getting Jaxson A Cell Phone

Once we became adults, Jaxson didn't really ask me for anything, so when he did ask, if I was able to help him I did. Jaxson called me one day and asked if I could help him get a cell phone.

Now during this time, I was married and my piece of husband got upset with me because I decided to add Jaxson to my T-Mobile account. He had the audacity to tell me that my brother never came around but he had the nerve to ask me for something. He felt that way because he was not able to try and use my brother, the way that he had done me. After it was all said and my ex-husband was a user and I thank God for that divorce.

I immediately let him know that whether my brother comes around or not if he needed my help and I could help him I would. I then reminded him that he was on my cell phone contract, so he needed to be quiet. During the time that Jaxson was on my contract he only paid his bill late once and that caused my cell phone to be turned off. I had to pay the bill, but he paid me back. Then Jaxson decided that he liked the cell phones that Sprint had better than T-Mobile. So he took his number and went to Sprint and that is where he remained until his death.

## ⌛ Jaxson Moved In with Me

I bought my first house in 2006; I signed my paperwork on July 21, 2006. October of that year Jaxson, called me and asked if he could stay with me for about 30 days. I said, "Sure." Little did I know his definition of 30 days and my definition of 30 days were totally different. While Jaxson lived with me I thought it would give us the opportunity to bond as brother and sister.

The first night that Jaxson moved in with me, I could see he was really hurt. He couldn't believe that our parents didn't want him moving with them. He said that they let Royce move with them and she was a free loader. I tried to comfort him as much as I could but, I knew at the time, I didn't want to see my brother on the streets.

It was an adjustment having him in my home, but it was okay. I felt like I was being a big sister like I was supposed to be. I also knew that I had to be firm otherwise; he would try to walk all over me. I told him that I would help him as much as I could.

## ⌛ Jaxson and the Three

I had heard thru the Grapevine that Jaxson had become a Whoremonger at the factory he worked at. I saw it first hand when he lived with me for those seven months. I also heard that working in a factory was like being at an all you can eat buffet. Jaxson told me that he messed with a lot of the women at the plant, because he could. When Jaxson first moved in with me he was dating Mechelle and dealing with Toni on the side.

As far as I knew Mechelle was his main girl. It was not always that way, somewhere along the way, Toni stopped being Jaxson's Main Girl and became his side one. Jaxson had become smooth with the ladies. He would drive Toni's car and have Roxanne it, Roxanne was another player in Jaxson's Game. One time in particular Roxanne's car broke down in front of my house and she was sitting at the table. Toni pulls up outside in her cousin's car. Jaxson met her on the porch, because he knew if she came in the house it would have been World War VI.

I understood the position that Roxanne was in because I had been there in my past, during my college days, after college and then with my low life ex-husband and that's why he's an ex now. Ain't God good he delivered me from that Emotional Hell.

Toni tried to hold on to Jax as long as she could but, when she got to the end of her rope, she didn't tie a knot in it and hold on, because he couldn't stand the past that she had. Now Mechelle was holding on for dear life, but after that birthday party, Jaxson stuck a fork in their relationship because he was done with her.

Somewhere along that line, Roxanne became the main girl, Jaxson decided that a bird in the hand beats any in the bush. The way that I remembered it was that Roxanne knew that she and Jaxson were creeping when they began their relationship. She crept long enough that she became his main girl and finally his fiancé. It was a long journey because she became his Fiancé' in 2009, that journey took 3 years. Roxanne withstood that foolishness and Jaxson chose her. It had to be serious because Roxanne was the only other woman that he lived with after he and Crystal got divorced.

I remembered a conversation that Jaxson and I had and he told me that Roxanne could make anything look nice. He really loved her and he was proud of their relationship. He said, "She was the Baddest in a good way". Based on the time that he lived with me I saw how he lit up when he talked about Roxanne after nearly 10 years of wrecking fury on the hearts of numerous women. Jaxson's heart had been tamed by Roxanne.

## ⌛ Jaxson took the Test

It had been a few weeks since he moved in and I noticed that he didn't like his job based on how he talked about it. I asked what was wrong and he said he wanted another job. I asked him what did he like to do, what he told me was what he didn't like and that was being around people.

Previously, I was a Corrections Officer, so, I asked him, "Would he consider that type of job?" and he said, "yes". So, I explained to him that once he took the test and passed it, he would get an interview and have to take his physical on the same day. He was okay with that. I also let him know that once he got his Black Tag, he could then become the Tower or the RV Officer, because those were 2 positions that had minimal people contact.

As the Tower Officer, he would spend 8 hours in the Rifle Tower, monitoring the perimeters of the prison and he would be able to see any suspicious activities that the inmates might be participating in. As the RV Officer, he would get to drive around the perimeter of the prison and make sure that no suspicious packages or people were trying to introduce contraband into the facility from the outside. Jaxson, said he was okay with that. I got him the application for that position and he completed the application and submitted it. He got his test date, took the exam and passed all of the parts needed so that he could be scheduled for an interview. His interview was scheduled and I tried to brief him so that he would know what to expect.

I was so excited for him the day came and I couldn't wait until he got home, so that he could tell me how the interview and the physical went. He walked in the door and I could tell by the look on his face that things didn't go well. I asked him what happened and he told me that he had forgot his wallet with his identification in it. He told me that the interviewer told him that he could reschedule his interview. I believe that he was truly disappointed in himself, because to my knowledge he never rescheduled his interview. I felt bad for him but I did what I could do to help him, the interview was his interview and not mines, so I couldn't make him pursue it if he chose not to and clearly he didn't pursue it because he never mentioned being scheduled for another interview.

## ⌛ Putting Jaxson Out

Little did I know the 30 days that Jaxson said he would need to live with me would turn into 7 months and by that time, I had enough and he had to go because, enough was enough. Of course when Jaxson moved in we had a conversation about him paying me rent to live with me. I asked him what he would be comfortable paying me for rent? He decided that he would be able to do $50.00 a week, I was okay with that. I didn't ask him to contribute towards the groceries because I was not going to let him be in my house and not feed him. My mother taught me never to begrudge someone of a meal of food and he wasn't just someone he was my baby brother. I thought it was funny because we hadn't lived together since 1998 after I graduated from ASU.

The only difference now was that I had Brad, my son. I thought it would be neat because Brad's dad wasn't an active part of his life and I thought Jaxson would be good a good example because, he worked every day and that was something that my son needed to see, that a man goes to work every day. So much for that idea because after while Jaxson's clothes were just at my house, when he didn't have a female to see he would lay his head under my roof. When the 30 days were almost up, he asked if he could have until after Christmas because he wanted to make sure that he was able to get his girls something for Christmas. I told him that was fine and then December turned into May.

By this time, I had enough, he wasn't paying me my rent like he was supposed to and it was in May right after his birthday, I told him that if my rent money was not underneath my pillow when I got home, I would be putting his stuff out and he better come get it. When I got home my rent money was not underneath my pillow, so I told him that he needed to come and get his stuff otherwise it would be in the yard. I was extending Tough Love.

He came and soon as he walked into my house, he had the audacity to tell me that I couldn't have it my way. I told him that my name was on the deed to my house not his. I further reminded him that he asked to live with me not me asking him to move in and I reminded him that it was supposed to only be for 30 days. I told him that I loved him because he was my brother, but I reminded him the only man that I was taking care of was Brad, my 6 years old son and not my grown brother. I told him I didn't love him unconditionally because I was not our mother and he was not my son, he was a grown man and not my responsibility.

When our mother found out that I put Jaxson out, she tried to give me a guilt trip, but I quickly reminded her that she created him and that he was not my son, he was hers. Although I put him out, I didn't love him any less, I just no longer wanted him in my house. I purchased my home for me and my son, not me, my siblings and my son. In my heart it was the right thing to do, because I had helped him as much as I could. Jaxson needed to find his own way, I couldn't find it for him and I was no longer going to be a hindrance to him.

# 5:45 A.M. - 6:45 A.M.

During a conversation with Momma, she gave her version of Jaxson's Last hour. Jaxson spent his last hour with our parents. I thought he wanted our parents to be the last people that he saw before taking his life because they were the first that saw him when his began his life. It is speculated that when an individual kills themselves in their parents' house, that is a sign of resentment towards his/her parents. I thought he wanted to go back home to the place where he felt most protected and knew that he would be looked after appropriately after he made the decision to take his life. Days before the Emergency Room Visit, on March 5th, 2012, Jax posted on Facebook, that he was going to be at the Pool Pub after work to play Pool and hang out, so anybody that wanted to come, show up.

## ⌛ Retracing His Last Steps

It was said that Jaxson spent his last evening on March 7th, 2012 at the Emergency Room with his fiance', Roxanne. Whatever the news was that the Emergency Room Doctor gave those two was enough to push Jax to making the decision that would change all of our lives. After he left the Emergency Room, Jax took Rox home and kissed her on her forehead and said, "I am going to see my Momma and Daddy, they stayed 2 blocks away. Jax walked on the porch and rang the doorbell it was about 5:15 a.m., Dewayne, our older brother answered the door because he was taking Diamond and Beauty home, so that Max, can take them to school. DeWayne moved back in with our parents, he was having a mid-life crisis and trying to find himself.

He told daddy that Jax was at the door. Jax picked up Beauty and Beauty told him that she wanted him to teach her how to play football, so that she could be a Football Star like he was in high school. She heard he was a Beast on the field when he played and Jax told her that they would work on it Saturday and that when the time came she wouldn't have to worry about getting tackled on the field. Beauty said, she wanted to play Flag Football because she knew she wouldn't get tackled and would not have to worry about getting hit. Jax, said ok, but you know Football is not a game for girls regardless of what you have seen on t.v.

Jax walked in and threw his car keys on the table and that was something that he never did. Daddy yelled and told Neicey that Jaxson was there. She yelled, from her room, "Here I come. As she walked out she asked, Jax, "What blew you this way early this morning?" He said, "I wanted to see my momma and daddy if that is alright with you?" Momma said, "Boy you know that you are always welcomed."

## ⌛ Jaxson and Momma

Jaxson had his last conversation with Momma. Jaxson, said, "Momma, that suit that I took pictures in, in February with Rox, when we went out, that's the finest suit that I have and that is the suit that I want to be buried in, in the near future." Momma, said, "Baby, what's wrong? Are you sick?" He said, "Momma, I don't know." Momma said, well is Rox sick?" Jaxson and Rox had been together since 2006. He said, "Hell something is always wrong with her."

Momma said, "Baby, what's wrong?" Jax said, "Momma, I am 36 years old and I ain't got S**t?" Momma said, "Son, you ain't never been in jail, you got a job and been there for over eight years, a car, a fiancé and three daughters." He said, "Momma, that is true, but it is not enough. I am tired; I have been working and busting my tail. I live paycheck to paycheck and it is no fun. You see you and daddy's living is made. You both just wait for the first, the third and the third Wednesday in each month to come and your money is in the bank. It does not matter if y'all leave the house or not; you both will still get your checks." Daddy looked at them in the dining room from the living room. Momma said, "Jax, talk to your daddy and Bay, talk to your son. Then she went in the bathroom."

## ⌛ His last Testament

Jax grabbed a chair form the dining room and sat really close to Daddy. As Jax looked into Daddy's eyes he began to give his last testament as tears fell down his cheek. "Daddy, if something happens to me, would you help raise my girls?" Daddy, said, "As long as they come around me, I will help raise them". Jax said, Jackie, his oldest daughter, didn't finish school and was busy chasing the video dreams, Jada, his second oldest daughter was hard headed and just would not listen. Now, Jocelyn, is going to be alright because she pays attention and listens and she has a good head on her shoulder.

Daddy, for a number of years I felt that you never loved me. I always had to compete with Matty for your attention. As I grew older I resented you for that, I didn't have the chance to get to know you like Matty did. I know that once Matty left for Basic Training, you attempted to build a relationship with me, but by then it was too late. I had a strong dislike for you. As I looked back I realized that you only did what you knew how to do and I don't know if I would have been in your shoes, having sons, if I would have done anything differently. I have daughters and yes Jackie is my heart but maybe it was different because they are girls and a father always wants to protect his daughters.

I learned that I should have embraced your efforts and maybe, just maybe my outlook would have been different. Now it really doesn't matter because I know what I have to do. As, I tried to understand why you were the way you were, I realized that you only did what you knew how to do. Whether our relationship was good or bad, you were there. You gave us something that I could not give my daughters, I was not a fixture in their lives and now I won't be. It truly hurts that

I did not make better choices and that I have given them memories that they will have to deal with.

Daddy, I want you to know that, "I know that you love me, but you loved Matty more, I accepted that and I love you because you are my daddy". I realized that you did the best you could and I wish I could have done better. He said, "I couldn't give them anything while I lived but they will have something, when I am gone." He then stood up and took a deep breath and walked towards the bathroom, but Niecey was in there, so he went into the basement.

While in the basement, he sat in the chair that he had placed against the wall and took off his shoes. Growing up, Daddy would always said, "A Man is not supposed to die with his shoes on." Momma, heard a loud pop. So, she called Jax by his Government Name, Jaxson Matthew Williams. She said, "Bay, I think Jax, shot himself." Daddy said, "Call the police." Deep down inside, Momma hoped that Jax accidentally discharged his gun and the bullet went into the floor, but because she knew that Jaxson, spent most of his time at the Gun Range once he got his CCW Permit, she knew that was not the case.

Before she walked toward the basement she asked God to give her the strength to do what she had to do, She went to the first set of steps in the basement and realized that Jax's gun not accidentally discharged. At that point she knew he had shot himself in the head because both of his hands were down to his side and blood was dripping from his fingers on his right hand.

Momma called the police and reported the shooting. Of course in Metro Detroit, when you call the police and report a shooting, they will send 7 or 8 police cars. While she waited for the Police to come, she called his siblings. By that time Dewayne returned from taking the girls to Max, so that she could take them to school. Dewayne said, if I would have stayed and talked to him, maybe I could have stopped him.

The police showed up and surrounded the house, Momma opened, the door and pointed in the direction of the basement. After the Police checked the crime scene and put up the Yellow Tape and the Coroner was called. While waiting for the Coroner to show up Jax's siblings arrived one by one: Maxine, Richard, Royce, Camden and Tabitha.

My mother, father and Dwayne were the only ones allowed to be in the house, while the Police completed the investigation of Jaxson's Suicide. It was very difficult knowing that a loved one took his or her life. The thought of suicide being committed is just something that is very hard to deal with, especially when you realized that there was nothing that you could have done to stop it.

The Coroner finally arrived, as she walked towards the house, Max hollered," Maybe I should blow my brains out too, and see if it takes the Coroner 5 hours to get from the Eastside of Detroit to here. Tabitha told her to calm down that the people from the Coroner's Office had to follow protocol. They finally brought Jaxson's Body out in the body bag on the gurney. It just seemed surreal, no matter how many times you watched that type of scene play out on television or in the movies, it just seemed different when it is someone you loved. Before they could move Jaxson's Body down the side walk, momma asked, "If she could pray over her baby's body before he was taken to the Morgue?" The Coroner, understood and Momma was allowed to pray over Jax's Body. Once she finished praying. Maxine kissed his feet and said, "My best friend is gone, he left me Lord, why?, now, what am I going to do?" She cried uncontrollably and her husband, Greg, grabbed her and held her in his arms. He said, "Max, baby, it's going to be okay."

Jax and Max, had an unbreakable bond, because they were twins. Max was 3 minutes older than Jax. Once they became adults, she began to call him her little big brother because she was older than him, but he was much bigger than her. Jax stood about 6'5 inches tall. Who would have thought looking back at that frumpy kid that he would have been that tall. Those two had worked for the same company for the last 10 years. They were both Hi-lo Drivers and they worked side by side. Jax drove Hi-lo # 12 and Max drove Hi-lo # 22.

Now, as they were putting Jax's Body in the Coroner's Wagon, our sister, Royce, fell on the ground and began to roll around, screaming, "Lord, God, why?, not my baby brother, take me, Lord." Tabitha, who is the baby, said, "If you don't get off of that ground looking like a fish out of water, I am going to wet you with the water hose." Royce, rolled and screamed. She didn't believe that Tabitha would wet her; and Tabitha did just what she said she would do. Everyone laughed, they were able to laugh at that moment and that was what was needed. Finally, Royce got off the ground and now she looked like a Spotted Cow. Everyone went into the house but Momma.

Momma stood in the middle of the side walk and watched the Coroner's Wagon as it drove down the street, until she couldn't see it anymore. She stood there for about 15 minutes, and finally Dwayne, put his hands on her shoulder and said, "Momma, let's go in the house, he's gone and all we can do is pray for his soul."

# The Call

I will never forget March 8th, 2012 as long as I live. It was a Thursday; I was at Wal-Mart getting two Straight Talk Cell Phones, because T-Mobile decided to cancel my contract at the end of the month. They sent me a letter telling me that my contract was being cancelled at the end of the month. I couldn't believe it I had been in Arkansas for over two years and now it was an issue with the towers. I was in the Electronics Department, I had picked out my phone and Brad's phone and it was 6:08 a.m., my cellphone was in my pocket and it was vibrating. My sister, Tabitha called, I answered and she yelled, but I couldn't understand her and she was calling Max's name. She was crying and I thought her husband had done something to her. After I said, "Hello," twice and she didn't respond. I hung up; I told myself I would call her later. Then my brother, Matty called, it was 7:15 a.m., before I answered his call, I said what the hell is everybody calling me for this early.

When I answered he was screaming and crying, "Jaxson killed his self," I said, "what Jaxson?" and he said, "our, brother.". I said," Let me call you back." I immediately called Momma and when she answered the phone, I said, "Momma, did Jaxson kill his self?" and she said, "Yes, a quarter to 7." I felt numb all over; I told Momma I would have to call her back. Mind you I am still at Wal-Mart with my 11 year old son, Brad, short for Bradford. He was at the other end looking at the games for his PSP. My eyes filled with water, I told him, to go find a cashier so that we could check out because Uncle Jaxson had just killed himself. I tried to call my best friend but she didn't answer.

Then I immediately posted on Facebook and asked for prayers for me and my family because my brother had just killed himself. By that time the cashier came, I picked out the cell phones and as I am leaving, Olivia, my best friend called me back and she asked which brother. She thought it was Matty and I told her that it was Jaxson and she asked me, "why" and I told her that, "I did not know." I told her I was on my way to the car and I would call her soon as I got in my car.

So, Brad and I got in the car and I put the keys in the ignition, and I began to scream and hit the steering wheel and," ask why?" then I said Lord, "Give us all the strength to endure this journey that we have to face." I then called my friend, Ms. Bettye, because she was a praying woman and I knew that she would be able to give me some encouraging words, but I couldn't get through. I began to talk to Brad and explain to him that we would still have to go on with our day and that I was going to work and that I was going to drop him off at school.

Before, I dropped him off at school; I asked him, "If he was okay?", and he said, "he wanted to stay with me" and I encouraged him to go to school. Once, I dropped him off at school, I immediately called my supervisor and he told me to stay home, I told him if I stayed home, I was just going to cry and that I had to stay busy. He didn't want to argue with me and he said ok, Dominique. I then drove to Hot Springs, which is where my brother, Matty lived. When I fanlly arrived at Matty's house, he was on the porch laid back in the chair crying with a co-worker and his girlfriend tried to comfort him. He got out of the chair and I got out of my ar and walked inside the gate and fell into his arms and cried like a newborn baby. I began having trouble breathing.

I was hyperventilating and I could barely catch my breath. Then Stephanie, my brother's co- worker, told me that I needed to pull myself together and that I needed to be strong for Matty.

I pulled myself together as best I could and then I drove down the street to my supervisors house and stopped by, his wife, Sonya, grabbed me and prayed for me and told me that it was going to be ok. My supervisor, Brian, said, we are here if you need us. I then made my way home to get my bag so that I could go to work. I couldn't find my keys that I had at Wal-Mart, but I did have an extra set.

I called to Wal-Mart and spoke to the guy in the electronics department and asked him about my keys, he told me that I had left them on the counter and I told him that I was on my way back to get them and he said that he would leave them at the Service Desk for me. Before I left home, I looked in the mirror and realized that my eyes were blood shot red from crying. So, I grabbed a pair of sun glasses and left to get my keys.

I called my preacher, Bro. Wallace, it was about 8:15 a.m., I told him that my brother killed his self and he asked was it anything that he could do, I asked for prayer for me and my family. Bro. Wallace, then said, he would call me back, because he was in a meeting at work. I called Bro. Turner and he asked if everything was ok and I told him, No. He asked what was wrong and I told him that my baby brother killed his self and then I asked him, if maybe there was something that I could have done to prevent this, He told me I did what I could, when I asked for prayers for my family in Michigan. I made it back to Wal-Mart and got my keys.

As, I left Wal-Mart, I decided that I would pick Brad up from school and speak to his Principle, Mrs. Rutherford and let her know what happened and that we would be leaving going to Michigan for my brother's Funeral. They informed me that Brad was scheduled to take a test Friday Morning and they suggested that I let him come to school to take the test and then I could pick him up once he was through with the test. Mrs. Rutherford, the Principal, Ms. Jones, Brad's Homeroom and Math Teacher and Mrs. May, the school Counselor, showed Brad and I care and concern during that difficult time.

I finally made it to work about 9:15 that morning, I told my co-worker, Marcus that I would be leaving to go home on Saturday and he asked if something was wrong with my folks. I told him that my baby brother had killed himself. He told me that me and my family were in his prayers.

As, I sat at my desk, I looked at my cell phone at about 1:45 p.m. and I saw that I had a voice message. It was momma, she had been crying and she said, "Nini, I got some bad news, please call. She Left me that message at 7:15 a.m., that morning.

I tried to do some work, but I just couldn't get anything done, I found myself crying and thinking about Jaxson and asking myself why. Then I would repeatedly say, "God give me he strength.".

It was during that time I began to lean on my faith and my relationship with God. During a conversation with my mother that day, I told her, that God knew when Jaxson left heaven, how he would leave earth and that if God wanted him to still be here, he would.

Late that night after I had finally fallen asleep, Momma called me; it had to be about 12:45 Midnight. She wanted to talk about Jaxson and I needed to listen. It was not possible for me to being there during the time that everyone else was there, I found comfort as I listened to Momma.

As she told me what happened, it allowed me to be there at that moment and for me that was what I needed. During the conversation, I asked Momma, "If the casket was going to be open, because I needed to see my brother one last time", and she never answered the question. I knew he had a number of guns, all different calibers, I was scared to ask which gun he used. Knowing what gun he used would determine the amount of damage that was done to his face and head. I found myself repeatedly talking to God and saying, "Lord, give us all the strength to endure this journey, position my steps so that I do not fall."

I realized that I was going home for a funeral and that would not be a Happy Occasion, yes, our family would be getting together again to celebrate Jaxson in death, but the sad part was that I don't remember after becoming adults that we ever celebrated Jaxson's Birthdays or the days that were special to him. Yes, we would be getting together to celebrate his life, but sadly he would not be there to enjoy it. Sometimes, when siblings become adults, they go their separate ways and the only time you do have a Family Reunion is at a funeral.

I decided that it would be best for me to drive home because this was an instance where I was not in a hurry to get home, but I had to go home. The drive was supposed to be almost 15 hours, but it ended up taking at least 20 hours. I decided that we would be getting on the road about 4:30 in the morning, I kept true to that. I honestly had not taken in to account, the stops for the bathroom, to eat, to stretch legs and to fill up for gas not to mention, there were 2 young people that were on the ride as well. So needless to say the ride took a long time, but that time on the road was definitely needed for me to continue on the journey to lay Jaxson to rest. I needed that drive to deal with his death and to prepare to see my family; I had not seen the majority of them since I moved to Arkansas in January 2012.

I was going to take the time during the drive home and reflect on the relationship that Jaxson and I had as adults. At that time, I was driving a 2003 Malibu and we all know that is not a large car.

I had not intentions on Matty, his girlfriend, whom he had been shacking with for God, knows how long and their daughter riding home with me, because I didn't want to deal with them at all, this would be my time to deal with Jaxson's death on my own, I would be able to grieve in peace.

Matty and his family are not small by any means, so it just made sense that he would drive his Tahoe, I told him, I would Google him directions and he could follow me. He told me that his car needed repairs and that I didn't understand why because he had not had a car note since November 2011.

I tried to be Diplomatic and tell him that the back of my car might be big enough for his daughter and my son, but an adult the size of his girlfriend would definitely be uncomfortable. At that point, I realized how selfish he was because he said, she would make that sacrifice to be there for him and that was fine and dandy but the shocks and springs on my car were not going to sustain all of that weight for the distance that we had to go.

Normally, when I traveled, it was just my son and I. We both knew the routine while on the road. So the thought of my brother, his girlfriend and their daughter riding in the car with us going to Michigan, didn't sit well with me because, they were all heavy hitters, weight wise and I didn't want my son to be uncomfortable during the ride to Michigan. Besides his girlfriend didn't care for me so, she did not need to be in my car. I explained to my brother that my car was not that big and that the ride would not be a comfortable one

Even, if they were willing to make that sacrifice for each other, I was not willing to make the frame of my car suffer nor my child be squished like sardines. God worked it out, her job at the Foam Plant wouldn't allow her to make the road trip because her and Matty were not married.

I was not complaining it was divine intervention, God knew that we were not going to make it being overloaded in a 2003 Chevrolet Malibu, I believed the weight capacity would have been about 1100 pounds, my son and I weighed the least. All I could think about was driving on the interstate and the car dragging and scraping the ground and sparks flying from the tailpipe, because it was too much weight for the car to handle and then we would have been stuck on the side of the road. Lord knows, at the time I didn't have AAA Road Side Assistance.

I drove the entire way home, I didn't want Matty driving my car because he drives to slow. Driving home allowed me to keep my mind on the road and I had to stay focused. I realized at that time, sometimes when you come from a large family, your family thinks you have to pick up the slack for them when they fall short. When you become and adult, you are responsible for your own family and not a bunch of grown folks that don't want to pull their weight.

I tried to remember the last time I saw Jaxson and I knew that it was before I moved to Arkansas. I moved to Arkansas, January 2010 for a job, because I had lost my job and couldn't find one there, so, I relocated to Arkansas with my son who was 8 at the time. I couldn't remember if I saw Jaxson in December 2009 or even in January 2010, but I did remember seeing him on Thanksgiving Day of 2009.

I stayed with my parents at the time and our brother, DeWayne was home for Thanksgiving and he invited Little Jackie, Jada and Jocelyn, Jaxson's daughters over. I remembered it so well because Jaxson was in the Dining Room at the table on Dewayne's Laptop. Jackie walked in the house and Jaxson looked at the coat she had on with a look of disgust. He asked her if that was the best coat that she had and then said, I bet your Momma got a better coat than that.

I thought to myself, if you wanted her to have a better coat go buy her one. At the time my parent's house was not big nor was it big enough for about 12 people at one time so, my son and I went to Momma Mitchell's and celebrated with the Mitchell's as usual.

During this time Jaxson and I didn't really talk, I believed he was still bitter because I had put him out of my house and I was still upset because he still owed me $85.00 since May 2007 and I knew that there was no chance of me getting my money now.

# The Drive Home

At the time of Jax's death I lived in Malvern, Arkansas. My older brother, Matthew lived in Hot Springs, AR. I realized that the drive would be longer than the 14 ½ hours and it should have taken longer because of the circumstances that required the visit home. Detroit, MI was my home town. My plans were to leave Saturday Morning, that way I could get everything in order on Friday, get me and my son's luggage packed and head out at about 4:00 or 4:30 a.m. Saturday Morning.

Now to my knowledge, my niece had not traveled on any long distance trips prior to this unplanned trip, but I also knew that my brother had not exposed her to certain things in her life, such as the etiquette of traveling. I was truly dreading the drive with my brother and niece because, I didn't believe that they could be in a car and be silent; because they are the types that had to hear themselves talk.

The fact that growing up, we were not really exposed to anything because our parents didn't take us anywhere, didn't surprise me that my brother hadn't taken his daughter anywhere. I told myself, while I was pregnant with my son, that no matter wha,t he would be exposed to things outside the city of Detroit. We would go on outings and he would know the proper etiquette for each situation. So, far my son had visited several didn't states and been exposed to various situations.

Boy was I right, my brother as old as he was at the time didn't think about the distance that we would be driving and the fact that I would need to concentrate while driving. I was now responsible for 2 extra people getting to Michigan safe and in one piece. Initially, the drive was fine, we talked about Jaxson and the different experiences that we shared with him. The things that were agitating was his daughter when, she was not sleeping, kept asking if we were out of Arkansas yet and the fact that my brother didn't know how to silence the buttons on his cell phone.

Now, while I am driving, I kept hearing the evidence of cellphone texts be received and sent. Finally, I asked him, "Did he know how to silence his buttons on his cell phone?" and he said, "He hadn't figured it out yet." I didn't understand that because he had that phone since August or September of 2010. I thought that he was truly remedial.

As we were driving I mentioned to him that Jax looked sick on his Facebook page. He told me that Jax had been working out. I told him that Jax hadn't worked out since before he stopped living with me because his ex-girlfriend Mechelle had gotten him a gym membership. Based on the pictures that I saw of him on Facebook, I believed he had gotten sick and didn't want to deal with the consequences of his action. The time frame from September 2011 to February 2012, Jaxson looked like he lost a lot of weight and his eyes were bulging out. So in my gut I believed that he had contracted H.I.V. and couldn't live with the consequences of his carelessness.

I didn't think that soon as we got him, Matty would tell the diagnosis that I gave him to our parents. They didn't need to know that, at that moment because they were suffering enough. I told him that he couldn't hold water and he talked too much. He tried to give me some excuse but I just didn't want to hear it. Now that the drive home was over, I dropped him and his daughter off and went to my best friend's house; she always had room for me and Brad. Olivia, was not just my best friend but she was my sister also. Olivia and I had been best friends since 7$^{th}$ grade at Durfee Middle School.

# PREPARING TO SAY FAREWELL

Preparing to say farewell to Jaxson allowed me to say farewell to Marigold Stephanie also. As, I prepared to say, farewell, I had to ask myself how do you say farewell to your baby brother?

Saying farewell to my sibling required that I allowed them to be laid to rest so that they could find eternal peace. I realized that the longer I moaned, hollered and called their names that they could not move on to the next part of the process after one has left the land of the living. I then thought to myself, how I would I feel if someone was holding onto my hand for 14 years and every time that I tried to move on they kept pulling me back. I realized that I would be mad as hell because they were forcing me against my will to stay some where I no longer needed to be.

Jaxson's Home Going Service was scheduled for Thursday. The visitation for his body was scheduled for Wednesday, from 3:00 p.m. - 8:00 p.m., but the family would be able to view the body beginning at 1:30 p.m. on Wednesday. When I got to the parking lot of the funeral home it was about 12:45 p.m., I immediately knew that the time had come and I finally would be able to lay eyes on my baby brother for the first time in over 2 years.

As I sat in that parking lot, I thought about the incident from 2 nights ago, when Matty and Royce had gotten into it over something so stupid, like who could do the splits. I didn't understand that by no means because they were both fat and both did the splits, those two were busy fussing over whose leg was the straightest and that made absolutely no sense. Now, they almost came to blows. Finally, Tabitha and I, told them both that, Jaxson did not fuss or fight and that we were supposed to be remembering him and that the way that they were acting was definitely not what he would have wanted. Jaxson was the type of person that would say what he had to say and do what he had to do and there was no place in the middle for all the extra who shot John or drama as some people would call it.

Sometimes during the death of someone who is African American, there will always be fussing, fighting and cursing. So, why was this funeral going to be any different? The majority of his siblings were pouring some liquor out in his remembrance. They were drinking every day. I told them if I was going to drink it definitely would not be with them and furthermore, Jaxson didn't even drink. Jaxson loved and smoked his trees on a daily basis; liquor just was not his thing. You see back in 1997, he got a hold to some liquor and it didn't sit well with him and after that to my knowledge he never tried it again.

Reality, set back in, Brad asked, "Momma, why are we just sitting in the car?" We finally got out of the car and went into the funeral home, that walk from the car to the door seemed like it was farther than a country mile and my legs felt like I had 20 pound weights on, my legs just didn't want to move. As I walked through the door, I laid eyes on Royce, she was pacing back and forth and her wig, looked like 10 miles of a bushy forest. It looked like the wig that Tina Turner wore in the movie, "What's Love Gotta Do with it", you could definitely tell that she got into a fight with some flat irons and the flat irons did not win. Due to the circumstances, she got a pass on that, I will attribute the state of her bad weave to the fact that her right mind had temporarily left because of the current circumstances.

Soon as Brad and I passed through the foyer, the tears began to fall; I didn't know what my brother would look like, all I knew is that he blew his brains out. The receptionist saw my state and gave me some Kleenex and she directed me to the room where my family was waiting. I saw Marsha, our older sister and Marigold's oldest sister. Marsha lived in Southfield and she had always been the voice of reason as well as being the Wind beneath my wings. We hugged each other and I began to cry on her shoulder and she whispered to me, "it is going to be ok." I nodded my head and said, "ok".

I found an empty chair and sat in it. I immediately began singing in a low voice one of the songs that we sang at church, "God allowed us to come together one more time, one more time, one more time, he allowed to come together one more time."

Bro. Gallagher, our Minister had come into have prayer with the family before we went in to view Jaxson's Body. As we are walking out of the room, I immediately began singing in a low voice again, "He allowed us to come together one more time, one more time, one more time, he allowed to come together one more time." The Bro. Gallagher began singing the song loudly, so we were walking down the hall singing that song.

As, we got closer to the room where Jaxson's Body was, Momma began to fall back, saying loudly, "He was my Flower, he didn't have to go like that, oh Lord, not my flower". Thank God that Matty was walking with her and was able to catch her, they both almost fell. Matty said, "Jaxson, wouldn't want to see you like this, Momma." I knew it would be difficult for her, because she lost a son and their birthdays were 1 day apart. I couldn't imagine the hurt that she felt nor would I want to I only have one child and he is my son. I am holding on to the thought that he will bury me and not me bury him, if it is God's Will.

As I stood over his casket looking at him, he looked peaceful he looked like he was sleeping. I couldn't see any signs of his brains being blown out, maybe it was the placement of the hat that he wore, but none the less he looked like himself.

Daddy was in a wheel chair, he was 85 at the time and because of the circumstances, it would have been difficult for him to walk, because he had one bad leg as a result of being in injured while he was in the war. I remembered after Daddy viewed, Jaxson's Body, he cried like a baby and said, "I wish I could have been a better father." When I heard my father say that, it tore me up in side. Yes, Jaxson killed himself but he was good and grown, our father and mother's job was done as it related to providing for us. We were all grown now.

I have viewed a number of dead bodies in my life and the expressions on their face told the story; whether they died peacefully or whether they died in pain, because they struggled with something before they passed on. As I looked at Jaxson's face, it appeared to me as though he had made peace with the decision that he made. At that moment I visualized him leaning his head back on the wall, closing eyes, putting his gun up to his temple on his right side, taking a deep breath and pulling the trigger. I also knew that when he made the choice that he made, he no longer cared about whatever possessions that he had and those things no longer mattered to him.

I had left the viewing at about 5:00 p.m. and then I decided that I would go back and sit with him until it was 8:00 p.m. because that is the time that the funeral home closed. I had a chance to see how loved he was, his co-workers and 2 of his companies Executives came and paid their respects. They told us that Jaxson was well respected and would truly be missed. We were also informed that the Hi-Lo Drivers on third shift gave a 21 Gun Salute using the Hi-lo's, that was a heartfelt gesture. I realized at that moment, I didn't know what it felt like to lose a son, but I sure as hell knew what it felt like to lose a brother and a sister and that pain was excruciating, worse than the labor pain I felt while I was giving birth to my son.

The morning of Jaxson's Funeral came, the family hour was scheduled for 1:30 p.m. and the service was scheduled to begin at 2:00 p.m. Bradford and I left Olivia's House at 11:00 a.m. It seemed like the moment that we got to my parents' house time slowed down. We were outside waiting for the car from the funeral home to come and get the family members that would be riding in the Family Car. Some guy in a car stopped and asked who was going to the prom and I told him that we were going to a funeral and besides I have never known any Proms to take place in March. That was just another reality check and it was painful.

While we waited for the car from the funeral home to come, I overheard Royce and Momma talking, they talked about the last couple of pictures that Jaxson had taken. They both said he looked like death was all over him. It has been said that your eyes are the windows to your soul and that you could tell a lot about a person through his or her eyes. I am not going to call anyone crazy. But what I will say is we are just not certified. I also wondered did they know something that we didn't and they had these special powers that allowed them to be Fortune Tellers? If they are they both need to be fired, because they couldn't see that Jaxson was going to kill his self. It's not like they were like Alice, from Breaking Down, at least she can warn Edward and the Cullens. But these two knuckleheads were sadly mistaken.

I realized I didn't want to be able to tell the future, because I would just mess it up. I wouldn't want that on my conscience and besides changing the destiny that God has created is impossible. The car from the funeral home finally arrived and we lined up in our cars. As we drove to the funeral home, this was one ride that I could have truly done without. I told myself that this would be the last time that I would be able to look at my brother in person and that was the bottom line. We drove onto the parking lot and we were directed to line our cars up in the formation that would be needed for the ride to the cemetery.

We all got out of our cars and began to line up in pairs of two outside the door leading into the sanctuary where Jaxson's Service would take place. We are lined up and Daddy was in the car crying and said, "I can't do this, I can't see my baby for the last time." Marsha' husband got the wheel chair out of the trunk and we took that long walk down that aisle. It seemed like we would never get to his coffin, I remembered the more I walked the more the tears fell, the day that I dreaded coming had arrived and it was nothing that I could do, but deal with it as best I could.

I remembered when Jaxson was younger and Royce had ordered some take out from Primos Pizza and Subs. Jaxson asked her to order him something and she said, "No". Jaxson told her that he was going to pull her wig off when the delivery man came. She paid him no mind, but just like he said, he kept his word. As she happily pranced to the door to pay for and get her food, just as soon as the Delivery Man handed her, her food Jaxson politely snatched that wig off. We all hollered, she slammed the door and the Delivery Man knocked on the door and said, "I just want my money".

As, I was walked down that aisle there were a number of scenes that were brought back to my memory about Jaxson. Like the time he kept bothering me, I was visiting for the weekend. During that time I lived with Marsha and her husband. I kept telling him to leave me alone, so finally after I got fed up with his silliness, I picked up a Scope Mouthwash Bottle and threw it at his head. He bent the corner before the bottle hit the wall. If I would have been a little quicker he would have been seeing stars. He could move when he wanted to. One of the jobs of a little brother is to be a pest at times and that he was at times, but I wouldn't have traded any of it for the world.

The funeral began, Tabitha and I wrote the program. So, I read the cards and acknowledgements and Tabitha read the obituary. I remembered Tabitha sounded like a Chihuahua, I knew it was only because she was emotional and trying to fight back her tears.

The order of service went as expected until Royce got up there with her bad wig and put on a show. Once she finished and walked of the stage, she tripped and fell, I thought, that's what she got because she was not on the program to speak anyway. Before Brother Gallagher began to Eulogize Jaxson, the family was given the opportunity to walk up and view his body one last time.

As we viewed Jaxson for the last time we returned to our seats and as they began to close the casket we lost it, I remember DeWayne's big burly self, grabbed and held me, talking about, I got you. I knew he meant well, but all I wanted to do was breath. I realized the only way I would be able to breathe again was if I got my composure together and I did that quickly. I knew it was difficult for Bro. Gallagher to Eulogize Jaxson because he had known Jaxson, since he was 5 years old and he looked at Jaxson, like a son. Bro. Gallagher's message was true and heartfelt and no one could have asked for anything more.

Bro. Gallagher completed Jaxson's Eulogy and walked down the aisle. Jaxson' Casket was then wheeled down the aisle and for the last time all eyes were on him. If Jaxson would have walked down the aisle, he would have done his infamous two step all the way down the aisle. Jaxson Matthew Williams was the Guest of Honor for the last time.

The saddest part is that we didn't celebrate Jaxson's Life while he was on these earthly shores and he did not get the chance to know what it felt like. As we walked behind the casket, it was very difficult to put one foot in front of the other or move something. That was one time in my life that I didn't want to move anything or shake what my momma gave me.

To see Jaxson's Coffin rolled into the back of that Hurst was surreal. Even though, I was there and witnessed the entire funeral, I just couldn't believe that we were at Jaxson's Funeral. The cemetery was on Plymouth Road in Plymouth, MI and the funeral home was on Plymouth Road and the Southfield Freeway in Detroit, MI; the funeral home was about five miles from the cemetery.

Jaxson did like the Cadillac Brand so it was only befitting that his final ride be in the Cadillac Hurst. The ride to the cemetery seemed to take 2 hours and we were only going 5 miles away. I remembered thinking that this was one destination that I wouldn't ask, "Were we there yet!" I knew that, that was a road trip that had to be taken and the destination could not be changed.

We made it to the cemetery, they wheeled Jaxson in the Mausoleum and the family came in and the grave side ceremony was completed in doors with the three roses being placed on the top of his casket. This is the first time that I had been in one of these since April of 2000 when my grandmother on Deniece's side passed away. So, we all got in our cars and we are leaving the cemetery or so I thought, I followed the Family Car and they were actually at the actual grave site. By the time I get to where the Family Car was I saw this big box, that I later found out was the grave liner and Jax's coffin was inside of the grave liner, so that the coffin wouldn't get destroyed.

The machine then lowered the grave liner in the ground and shove the dirt right over it and covered the hole, that was Jaxson's Final Resting Place on earth. When it was done, I said, "That's not how it's done on t.v., I thought we would get to throw dirt on his coffin once his coffin was lowered in the ground?" I learned that everything that happens on t.v. does not happen in real life.

We left the cemetery and headed to the church for the re-pass. As I drove to the church, I kept thinking, Jaxson's in that box and he can't breathe and that they really needed to let him out or he was going to suffocate. In my mind I knew he was dead but at that moment I tried to hold on to that last thought of this being a bad dream and I changed the ending. I was never more wrong in my life. I wanted to change God's Plan; I wanted my baby brother to still be on this side of time. That was the selfishness in me and God's word made me realize that it was not to be and that trying to being selfish didn't matter because God let us all know that Jaxson's Work was done here.

I finally made it to the church to eat and I was glad because I was so hungry that my stomach was talking loud. As the family was eating, all you heard was, "F* * * her loudly, Royce figured out that Toni a friend of the family's daughter had brought some liquor into the church and Momma, told her to take it outside. So, the comment was made towards our mother. Royce hops up trying to charge like a big bull blowing smoke and trying hit a target. DeWayne grabbed Royce, I swore it looked like that bad weave was trying to get away from her head; and Charles, Tabitha's Husband blocked the door and I said, "This is not the time or the place, we are supposed to be honoring Jaxson's Memory, so please let us do that!"

I took my seat, so that I could finish eating and Bro. Gallagher sat at the table and said, "We figured something was going to happen." I said, "Yep." You see when we were younger the Williams Children were always doing something and it was said that something's that you do, stay with you for the rest of your life. All I knew was that I was not a child anymore and I didn't my son to see me act like I did when I was a child, because now, I am a woman and a mother. It was true that the Williams's couldn't have an event where no one acted stupid or there was fighting or an attempted fight.

Jaxson had been laid to rest, now I had to begin the healing process. I knew the journey would not be easy but it was a journey that was needed. So, I began to do some self-re-evaluating. I had to make sure that the fruit I was bearing was good and not rotten to the core. I knew that once your eyes close to open no more, you will be remembered by the fruits that you bore and it didn't matter if it was good fruit or fruit that was rotten, rotten is rotten no matter how you sugar coat it.

# DEALING WITH THEIR SUICIDE

## ⌛ Calling it what it is

When someone commits suicide, often times people will try to tip toe around the fact that the individual took his or her life, regardless of the method that was used, they still committed suicide. Suicide is defined as the act of taking one's own life intentionally and voluntarily. You have to call Suicide, just what it is and you cannot call it by any other name, but suicide. You see it's one of those things that no matter how you try to soften it up it stays, hard, cold, callus, thoughtless, selfish and non-caring.

Suicide forces you to question yourself, it makes you look deep into your soul to find out, if you were a contributing factor to the act that your loved one committed it forces you to be honest with yourself. Yes, it would be much easier if they would have died in a car accident or a drive by shooting, because then you would be able to say that it was a random act. Unfortunately, this

was clearly not the case, It was not until after Jaxson killed himself that I thought about the way that Marigold died. I then realized that they both committed suicide, hers was a result of many years of drug use and Jaxson's was a self-inflicted gunshot to the head, he intentionally took his life. In his case I wanted to think that after he pulled the trigger he realized what a mistake he made, but that was not hardly the case.

You see I tried to put myself in his shoes and go through the motion without having a gun. You see if I was going to commit suicide, first of all I would not shoot myself anywhere because I would not mess up my head, face or chest. Just think, you decide to kill yourself and you are going to use a gun. Well, guest what soon as you pull the trigger and the bullet leaves the chamber, you cannot take it back nor can you say whoops it was an accident, why, because your dead no sooner than the bullet enters your body and the only way you're not, is if the gun miss fires or jams, but what is the likely hood of that happening.

I would not stab myself or slit my throat because that would inflict pan and I am just not going to do it. I do not want any blood all over me. I would not do it using my car, because just my luck, the car would blow up, once it crashed and my body would be burned and I would not be able to have a funeral service, because my body would be ashes. I would have to have a memorial service because there would not be a body for anyone to view.

Furthermore, I have three reasons why I would not commit suicide: one, my body does not belong to me, it belongs to God; two, I am not able to replace my life once I take it and three; I have a son to take care of and think about. You see, when I became a mother, God gave me something that was more important to me than anything in this world. I would not want my son to go through the rest of his life wondering why I didn't love him enough to stay around. I am not knowingly going to inflict that type of emotional pain on my child whom I love dearly.

Furthermore seeing the pain that two parents caused their children is a pain that I would not knowingly or willing inflict on my child. I realized that they both took the coward's way out, because they took something that was not theirs to take, they stole from their family and most of all, they stole their children's mother and their children's father. At that point they were very selfish and cared about no one but themselves. Yes, Marigold was on dialysis, to my knowledge she did not reach out for help and I now know that when you have an addiction often times you are not in your right mind and the feelings or thoughts of others are the farthest thing from your mind.

In order to move past Marigold's death, I had to realize that she was tired and was never happy and to live your life day after day, not being happy living or having a peace of mine is like living in captivity. The drugs had her mind and the drugs caused her to lose her soul.

As it relates to Jackson, whatever it was that he was going through or discovered that he had, there was no reason to take his own life. With the advancement of medical treatments today;

there are resources that are available to help a person deal with just about anything, but suicide was not the answer. I realized that once Jaxson became an adult, he was very selfish and had a sense of entitlement, but what he failed to realize is that once you become an adult, "nobody owes you anything, if you don't work and earn it, then you won't get it."

I realized that when Jaxson shot himself in our parent's basement, he wanted to make them hurt and feel the pain that he was feeling. I was told that when a person kills themself in their parent's house, it could mean the following: one, they resented their parents and killed themselves in their parents' house to get back at their parent's and make them feel hurt. Two, they killed themselves in their parent's house because, they wanted to be in a place where they were loved.

To our knowledge, neither one of them had a mental illness that caused their thought process to be off. At this point, I realized that their time had come and they had to go and that is the way it was going to be. In each and everyone's book of life God authored the beginning and the ending and it is truly out of our hands.

As I thought about the relationship that my brother and I had, I was saddened. Now that he is gone, we can't work on having a better relationship. His suicide was a tragic event; that made me look at the relationship that we had. In every relationship someone has to be the bigger person.

After all, I was one of his older sisters and I should not have let my pride get in the way of us having a true relationship. It is not always about who is right or who is wrong; it is about having respect and admiration for your loved ones. Yes we were siblings, but we were not friends.

In dealing with their suicide, it made me look at my life and see what I needed to do differently. I want to live the rest of my life making a positive difference. I want to know that at the end of the day, I affected someone's life in a positive manner. If there is a time when I hurt someone's feelings or crossed a line that I should not have crossed, I will do what I am supposed to do to make it right. I know that not everyone is going to like me, but I know as long as I am not harming anyone and I am living my life as God requires, I will be just fine.

# Speculation Lingers

Roxanne and I were always cordial with one another. I didn't believe that there were any ill- feelings or animosity between the two of us. I wanted to clear my conscience about the reason I believed that my brother took his life; Jaxson, Roxanne and God knew the reason why.

Jaxson was not and I repeat not talking. I hoped that God would allow it to be revealed to me through Roxanne the reason why Jaxson was no longer here and that's only if she feels like talking and if not; I pray that God will convert me so that I may find peace with my brother's death.

I have always believed that there are certain conversations that need to take place face to face and this would definitely be a face to face conversation. Roxanne agreed to meet me at the Bone

Yard, Jaxson loved that restaurant and the ribs were not too shabby. I knew this meeting would be a difficult one, but I wanted to talk to her without my siblings being around. I would let her know my thoughts and hopefully that would be enough for her to give me the answers that I needed to find closure about my baby brother killing himself.

She showed up and our conversation began. I informed her that the last time I remembered laying my eyes on Jaxson was before I moved to Arkansas, other than that we didn't talk and I was not aware of what was going on in his life or their relationship. I let her know that when

I looked on his Facebook Page that he looked sick to me and that he had lost a lot of weight during a short period of time. I told her that I believed that he had contracted HIV and didn't want to live with it or the embarrassment. I also told her that I believed the reason why he didn't kill himself in their house was because he didn't want her to kill herself.

Roxanne let me know that she had been with Jaxson since 2006 and that she loved him dearly and that he loved her. She indicated that when they got together; they both brought baggage to their relationship. She said she realized that Jaxson would always love Crystal because she was his first love and the mother of his children, but that didn't mean that he didn't love her. I realized that Jaxson was not happy about his divorce all though he accepted it, he didn't get married to get divorced. He wanted to be an intricate part in his daughters lives but when the divorce came, what he wanted was thrown out of the window.

She said over the years Jaxson shared information about our family and his childhood and he was unhappy about the life that he had made for himself and he just saw no way for it to get better.

She informed me that Jaxosn told her about the 2 nervous breakdowns that our mother had and that it was a possibility that he had issues that he needed to deal with but going to see a Shrink was not in his plans.

Roxanne made it very clear that during their relationship that Jaxson stepped up to the plate. He began to provide for their household. He paid the bills and worked over time and sold his beloved Cadillac to get their lights turned back on after he found out that she wasn't paying the bill. He was tired of struggling and living paycheck to paycheck. The stress of everyday living got on his back and he figured a way to get it off of his back.

She made it very clear that when Jaxson tried to establish a relationship with Jada, his second oldest daughter that went out the window quickly and the fact that Jackie hadn't finished high school really bothered him. Roxanne knew that Jaxson Matthew Williams was voted most likely to succeed by his Senior Class and when he looked back on his life, he saw repeated failure. He didn't see success anywhere in his life.

Jaxson didn't think that never going to jail or being incarcerated in the Prison System was a success. He didn't see that graduating from high school prevented him from being a statistic and that did make him a success, he didn't see what society defined as success; the big house or luxury cars, along with a big checking account. He didn't realize that his failures of yesterday he could have made his successes of today and tomorrow.

He did not realize that his childhood and past were meant to be steps that he needed to climb during his journey in life; that would eventually get him to the point where he could see success beyond his wildest imagination. Somewhere along the line Jaxson never had that conversation that would have told him that the things in life will either make you or break you depending on how easy you want to give up or how hard and long you want to fight. Because the only time your life gives up on you is when you give up on it.

Before our conversation ended Roxanne let me know that while Jaxson was alive they kept their relationship between the 2 of them and she saw no reason to change that since he was gone. She made it very clear that she was going to keep the memory of their relationship between them. I had to respect that and I respected the love that they shared.

So after it was all said and done Roxanne did not confirm whether he did or didn't have HIV. Roxanne said, "If Jaxson wanted his family to know what was going on with him, he would have shared the information". It was evident that he did not want us to know, because he did not leave a note nor did he tell us. She made it very clear that whatever if anything Jaxson had; he took it with him to his grave and that was where it needed to stay. I then realized that I would have to find closure on my own.

## Being Angry

Yes, I was very angry at both my brother and sister, because they decided that their lives were not worth living and the love that they had was not strong enough to convince them to stay; and make the needed changes to be the wonderful people that at one point in their lives they were.

Being angry is necessary to deal with the fact that they killed themselves. There is no set time frame on being angry. I just knew that being angry forced me to admit that I am human and that I had feelings and my feelings were hurt. I realized that the reason, I was angry was because I lost my loved ones.

I knew that directing my anger towards someone else would not have been fair nor was it going to help my situation. I told myself why I was angry at them both. There were several reasons for me to be angry at Marigold and Jaxson. Neither one of them loved themselves enough to fight and regain the life that they once knew. They allowed darkness to move right in and kicked the sunshine out. Sunshine gives everyone a reason to smile and continue on. They ignored God's invitation to have a wonderful relationship with him. (1st Peter 5:7—Casting all your care upon him; for he careth for you).KJV

When you have a relationship with God that does not mean that you won't suffer or have trials and tribulations, what it means is that God will make each and every situation bearable and he will give you the strength to endure. As a result of my relationship with God and my spiritual beliefs, I had to ask God to forgive me for being angry with them both. God made me realize that it was not about me and their deaths were necessary in order for my faith and dependence on

God to grow stronger. When Jaxson killed himself, I asked Marsha why and all she could say was I don't know. I found myself continuously asking God for strength and thanking him for the time that I had both of them in my life. I realized that being angry was not healthy for me and I did want that anger to cause me to age before my time. I stopped being angry and it is because I was able to call on the name of Jesus during my darkest hour.

# Allowing Myself to Grieve

I asked myself the question, "Why do I need to grieve?" I attended my first funeral service when I was 7 years old. One of my older cousins had passed away, as a result of not receiving a Blood Transfusion; and after a serious injury in an automobile accident. His wife was a Jehovah Witness and she said that, "It was against their religion to receive blood transfusions." I know I was only 7 at the time but I still had common sense enough to know that I had not read or been told that there was anything in the New Testament that did not allow for Blood Transfusions; nor does the New Testament tell Christians to call themselves Jehovah Witnesses.

Now that was my first time experiencing the death of a loved one, yes, he was my cousin but he was an older cousin and my thought during that time was to find someone that looked friendly and sit next to them after all we were all family. At the age of seven I had no idea the meaning of grieving, as the years progressed I continued to lose loved ones, and I knew that when they passed that their time was up because they were either sick, never fully recovered from a stroke or slept away from here, they died in their sleep.

By this time I knew the reason that those relatives died, I knew my mother's mother was sick and I knew that when she left the hospital that the doctors had informed her that there was nothing else that could be done for her. I was at peace with her dying because I knew that there was nothing else that could have been done to save her life. I saw my Grandmother two days before she passed away and I knew that she knew I loved her and I knew that she loved me, I would have loved to be there to see her the day she went to slumber. I was at peace when she passed away because I didn't want her to suffer. By the time we found out she had cancer, she was terminal, and the cancer had spread throughout her body.

To know that Cancer is a carcinogen and just eats away at a person's organs until they can't function and are in an enormous amount of pain. I found comfort in knowing that my grandmother would not have to suffer anymore. Was, I sad when she passed, without a doubt, but in my heart at that time I knew she was not in any more pain, she lived to get 73 years old and that was a blessing. God's word tells us if we are obedient unto him, we will get 70 years.

***(Psalm 90:10: The days of our years are threescore years and ten; and if by reason of strength they be fourscore years, yet is their strength labour and sorrow; for it is soon cut off, and we fly away.)***

I knew I would miss her, but I had found comfort in knowing that I had a chance to see her one last time before she passed away. It was easier for me to accept her death because it was expected that you would bury your Grandparents and Parents. What is not expected is that you will bury a younger sibling or older sibling especially when they are still young. The reality of it was that I did have to bury my siblings, so then I was left with trying to figure out what grieving would allow me to do?

Grieving is something that is done to allow the loved ones to deal with the death of a loved one and to heal from the loss that has been suffered. I also knew that the healing could not and would not begin unto the grieving process was over. So, then I asked myself, how long am I supposed to grieve and whatwas the protocol for grieving? I didn't know if I have grieved right or long enough?, especially when as a child, I was not made to understand that dying is a part of living and living is a part of dying. Surely as we are born we must die, that is the process that God created. I have since learned that the living does not truly begin until death has occurred on this side of time. My relationship with God has given me comfort because in the Bible it clearly states that: “[(27] And as it is appointed unto men once to die, but after this the judgment:.” (Hebrews 9:27).

God’s word is not a lie, so I knew that was true because it is stated in the bible. I have learned that I am not to ask God why, but to ask him for the strength to endure the journey that must be taken when a loved one has passed on and the ability to move forward. I have learned that all things are possible through Jesus Christ, because he provides the strength that is needed to move forward in due time. Accepting that they are gone and are no longer amongst the land of the living is required in order for my healing process to begin.

I have accepted that they are gone from this side of time. I know that God made no mistakes and that I had an opportunity to have Marigold as my sister for 25 years and she never treated me bad or did me wrong. She was an older sister to me and for that I am grateful and I thank God for that. Jaxson, was my baby brother and I had him in my life for 36 years, no they were not always the best of times but they certainly were not the worst of times either. If those times that we had, had not happened, we would have not gotten to the place that we arrived at and for that I am truly grateful.

# LETTERS SAYING GOODBYE

Dear Marigold,

*Marigold I have decided to write you this letter because there are something's that I wanted to say to you but you are not here, the next best thing is to put it in this letter. I know that once I have written this letter, I will have closure and my grieving process for you will have ran its course.*

*I wanted you to know that sometime during the month of December 2007, while I was working for Camp Oakland and I was going to Aunt Tina's house, I thought that I saw you walking down Huron Street, so I doubled back around the corner to see if it that was you, I don't know why I just didn't back up, but what I do know is that when I came back around the corner you were nowhere to be found.*

*We hadn't seen each other in over 11 years, so I know that you did not know the type of car that I drove and I didn't know if you thought that I was someone that wanted to hurt you; but I wasn't, I was a younger sister that thought she saw her older sister and just wanted to make sure.*

*I got the call on March 13th, 1998 that you were dead, I immediately thought back to that night that I thought I saw you and because I was not able to see if it was actually you, it has bothered me for the last 14 years. I want you to know that I love you and miss you dearly. I have a son and his name is Bradford, but we all call him Brad. I have told him all about you and no matter what you were always a big sister to us and that you wouldn't let anyone bother us. There were three incidents in particular that I told him about and he just found it so hilarious. The first incident was when Matty was little and that boy named Arthur, was picking on him you beat him up andArthurs's mother came tour house and asked, "Mrs. Williams why her Marigold was picking on her Arthur and Marigold, boldly said, "tell your Arthur to stop picking on my brother."*

*It was so funny because to see you run out of the house and your hair was just flowing with the wind, I don't know if you were trying to keep up with your hair or if your hair was trying to keep up with you. After that Matty, did not have any more problems with Arthur.*

*The second incident was, when Dewayne and you were playing the dozen and you told Dewayne that freaks came out at night and you told him that he looked like a freak and we all started laughing. Then Dewayne got so upset that he poured water on you. Then you told Daddy and soon as Daddy went back into his study, you told Dewayne, "throw some more damn water and Daddy would be throwing you out because you were going to beat his you know what."*

*The last incident was when you were staying with us in Detroit and I was in the 8$^{th}$ grade and attending Durfee Middle School and I would come home and sometimes my hair would be messed up and sometimes it wouldn't. You realized that on the days that my hair was messed up that I must have been doing work and would scratch in my head when I was thinking in class and doing my work. So, the last day that you were in Detroit and I came home, you asked me did I do any work at school and I told you, "Now", and you responded, "I figured that because your hair is still in place," then you busted out laughing and I just looked like a deer in headlights. After you said that I began to pay attention to see if it was actually true and I realized that it was and all I do is laugh when I think about that.*

*I still do the same thing, 25 years later. Now, Brad mentions that to me when I come home from work, he gladly says, "You must have worked real hard today ?" I don't even have to look in the mirror, I immediately burst out laughing.*

*When you passed, I didn't know what to do or think, I just felt in my heart that you were still supposed to be here with us. I know that I had no control or say over your life, but I wanted you to know that God has provided me the strength to move forward and I know that moving forward does not mean that I have to forget about you. All though you have passed on, the memories that you left me with, have provided many impressions that I carry with me wherever I go. I want you to know that even though you are gone, you are definitely not forgotten and you left some funny memories and for that I want to say thank you.*

*Love Your Sister*

*Dominique*

---

Dear Jaxson,

*I write this letter to you because there are something's that I wanted to say to you. I can't*

*Physically say them so I had to write them, even though you are gone, I know that you will read this letter.*

*It was so ironic because on March 6$^{th}$, I was thinking that it would be 14 years since Marigold passed on March 13th, which was exactly one week away. I could not believe how the time had flown. Then I asked myself, "I wondered which one of us would be the next one to die?" Little did I know that in two days you would give me the answer to that question! I wanted to know, but I didn't want to know, if that makes any sense. That's why you have to be very careful of the things that you ask for because most of the time God will give what you ask for.*

*It took a minute to register and then after, I realized that you were really gone because you had shot yourself in the head. The first thing that came to my mind was that selfish mother* * *r. It seemed like once you got divorced, your thought process changed; I don't know if it was what happened during your marriage that affected you or if you honestly* *believed that the world owed you something. I surely hoped that was not the case because once we become adults, the world owes us nothing, our parents job is done and if we don't work and earn it, then we don't get it.*

*I remember during a conversation with Momma, she said that, "You looked like the Walking Dead and that you were not taking care of yourself." Little did she know that you were slowly dying because of the choices that you made, you thought with the wrong head and got something that you couldn't get rid of, at least that is what I believe based on how you looked to me. You see when I looked at your pictures on Facebook, I thought you had got something and were sick, but I also knew that with the breakthroughs in medicine today, you could just about live with anything except for when your illness is in a terminal stage. I want you to know that I spoke to Roxanne and she told me that whatever was going on in the inside of your body was between you and God and if you wanted your family to know your personal business you would have told us. She also said that since you didn't tell us anything that it was not her place to tell your business. I respected the fact that she respected you in death, so I couldn't be upset or angry even though, I can only believe what I believe but without a confirmation it is just my belief.*

*I do understand the reason why you didn't kill yourself in the house you two shared together because you knew that she would have killed herself too and maybe just maybe you could not bear the thought of her taking her life because of what you had done to her emotionally. You two had lived together since 2009 and were supposed to be in a monogamous relationship but it is quite apparent that you were not. You couldn't be honest with her because you still harbored feelings from your past that you hadn't dealt with.*

*I have spent the last few months trying to make sense of your actions. I have finally realized that nothing happens without God allowing it to happen. Because God is in charge of it all and I didn't have a say in the matter anyway. So, finally after I realized that there was nothing that I could have done to stop you from blowing your brains out; I now realize that I have to be a better me so that I could live my life to the fullest. I thank you because of your actions, I had to re-evaluate my life and make sure that everything in my is in order. Your untimely death has made me realize to take nothing and no one for granted.*

*I remember the day of your Funeral, I stood over your casket and looked at you one last time, I really wanted to slap the crap out of you, but then I remembered you were dead and there was not any crap in you. Then, I wanted to slap the taste out of your mouth, but dead people can't taste anything. I wanted to knock the piss out of you, but once again dead people don't have any bodily fluids, because they are dead. I just really wanted to beat you like you stole something because of the indescribable pain that you had caused me to feel. Then I realized if I had done that, I would have had to fight our family; I would have then got arrested for abuse of a corpse and I didn't want another set of handcuffs on me, that first and last pair that I had in August of 2009 was enough. Just in case you have not figured it out, I was really angry at you and I wanted to take my anger out on you but it would have done no good because you are dead.*

*It has definitely taken me some time to get over the anger I had for you because, you cheated us all. I remember when I saw you Thanksgiving 2009, I don't remember if I saw you during the Christmas or New Year Holiday, I don't even remember if I saw you before I moved to Arkansas but, I remembered that last Thanksgiving that I was home. I was looking forward to coming home for Camden's Graduation and I was going to roll my eyes at you and go about my business, but you stole that opportunity from me. I wanted you to walk me down the aisle when I got married again, but you cheated me of all that. I wanted to call you and tell you how your nephew was doing in sports, but you took that opportunity from me and it hurt so bad that I could feel it in the pit of my stomach.*

*I know that at one point you had a wonderful heart but somewhere along the way during your life's journey, something happened that caused your heart to change. If I could have done anything that would have caused you to change your thought process, I would have, but like the old saying goes, when you don't know, what can you do?*

*I want you to know that Brad is playing football and the coaches say that he is going to be awesome as long as he keeps progressing. While I was watching him play this season, I told myself that he got some of those skills from you and that the times that he made those touchdowns and tackles, you were there. I realize that I can no longer be angry at you because, it was your time to depart the land of the living. I had you for 36 years and for that I am grateful, I want you to know that I miss you and I love you. I will hold onto the memories that we shared because that is what you left me with and that beats not have any memories at all.*

*Love Your Sister,*

*Dominique*

# FINDING CLOSURE

I have learned that in this life as long as I live all things that come to an end need closure.

Closure is necessary for the healing process to be completed. Closure allows you to put an end to a part of your life that is now over and it enables you to move forward. Obtaining closure is not always cut and dry; often times there is baggage, pain, the lack of understanding and emotional hurt that comes along with trying to obtain closure. My baby brother, Jaxson Matthew Williams killed himself on March $8^{th}$, 2012 and that day my life changed forever. I realized that nothing in life should be taken for granted, no matter how big or small, everything and everyone has a value. Value does not always mean monetary, things and people always have value to someone.

I looked at the relationship that my brother and I had, I realized that we were not close, I knew he loved me and I loved him because we were brother and sister but that was it. Once we became adults our focus was what was going on in our individual lives and there was little room for each other. We didn't always agree with each other but at the end of the day we were family and when all else fails you still have your family. The sad part was I never told him that I loved him while he was living and now I can't tell him in death because his ears don't hear anymore.

Knowing that my brother killed himself is painful and it hurts more than those back labor pains that I had while giving birth to my son. The thought of him taking his life because of his life experiences cut deep and hurted like h*l*. I had to look at my life and find value in everything that I have experienced, whether it was good or bad but none the less it has allowed growth, triumphs and victories. Our views were different and I never walked in his shoes, so I don't have the right to be angry or upset with him because he decided to take his own life. Initially, I believed that I should have been angry and upset with him because he was my baby brother and he was supposed to be here. Jaxson chose to do what he did and I was nowhere in the equation, it was not about me. I realized that he did what he felt was best for him. You see, I was not in his head, so I did not know what he was dealing with. What I do know is that got loaned Jaxson to me for 36 years and when his season was over, it was time for him to leave.

I realized that my brother was in pain and the pain became unbearable and he chose to end the pain by ending his life. I will always love and miss him, but I will never forget him. I can no longer be angry or upset with him because of the choice that he made, I am not his judge nor his jury. Holding on to that pain and that hurt was not allowing me to move forward, I was tired of going through the motion, I was stuck in emotional quick sand after my brother passed. I was angry with him and I wanted to inflict pain and anger on someone else because he took his life. I didn't want to smile any more, I just wanted to be evil and mean towards people because of what my brother had done to me or so I thought. I knew in my heart and mind that the person that I was angry with was not here, so there was no need to direct that anger towards someone that had nothing to do with my brother taking his life.

My faith and my spiritual growth would not allow me to be evil or mean because I knew that everything that happens God allows it to happen. We are all supposed to find the good in every situation no matter how difficult or hard it might appear to be. I found myself struggling, although I know what the Bible tells me and I dare not argue with God's Word or try to change God's Plan.

I was on my Spiritual Journey with God before losing my brother, but because this death hit close to home, it has allowed me to draw closer to God, Jesus Christ and his word I realized that I was being selfish and that my brother didn't belong to me, he was loaned to me, we all belong to God. God is a parent and with any parent, when you are ready for your child to come home after they have been out playing. He will do two things: call that child and wait for that child to come home and if that child does not come home he goes and brings his child home, when they have played enough, like any Good Parent, God knows best. Jaxson Matthew Williams was born and he died because his journey had ended, his time was up. My time of grieving has come to an end that season is over now, I have closure and now I can move forward, because of God's Grace and Mercy.

# This Journey is Completed

As sure as each journey begins, it must come to an end. This journey for me began on March 13th, 1998 and it has taken almost 15 years for me to complete. I had to deal with the loss of two siblings: an older sister and my baby brother in order to complete this journey. Looking back nothing about our lives was easy; some of us chose to stick it out and overcome the obstacles that were placed in our paths by our parents. Some of us are still fighting with those obstacles on a daily basis. While, others chose to end the struggling and the fighting with the everyday factors of life. When individuals commit suicide that does not mean that they were less of a person, it just meant they chose to end the suffering on the inside that no one else could see on the outside.

This journey forced me to look at some issues that I thought I had dealt with years ago.

What I had done was put those issues in a mental trash bag and chunked them in the back of the closet in my brain. Prior to my brother killing himself, I was reflecting on my life and the decisions that I had made and I went through all of the should haves, could haves and would haves that I equated to a Roller Coaster Ride. I realized that those things were not going to change anything that I had done because they were a part of my past. I realized that everyone has a past and the past is filled with good and bad memories, but if the things in the past had not occurred then we would not be the individuals we are today.

Prior to looking on my brother's Face Book Page and I getting the news that he took his life. I thought back to something that Jaxson said years ago. I remember him saying that he didn't want to live to get past 40. Now I wonder if he knew something that we didn't know, but none the less he didn't live to get 40. You have to find the good in every situation, no matter how difficult it may seem.

I now understand, that each and every person on God's Green Earth will have to ride on the Roller Coaster of life that has been appointed by God so that we can get to our individual Destination. When you look at the roller coaster ride, you can blatantly see that there are ups and downs, I have yet to see a roller coaster ride that does not go up and down; so, why should our lives be any different?

In our lives we can't predict the future and we sure cannot change the past. Remember the old saying, "If it doesn't kill you it will make you stronger"? During this journey, I realized that my past does not and will not define me as the woman that God has allowed me to become. At one point or another during this journey, I had allowed myself to be consumed with my past guilt about my relationship with my two sibling. One day, I realized that my past was just that and I am no different than anyone else because we all have a past.

I don't know anyone whose past is their present; those two entities will never cross paths, because they were not meant to. The light bulb finally went off; I could not comfortably live in the present because I was holding on to my past. All this time my back was sore and my shoulders were bruised because of the luggage that contained: hurt, heartache, pain, tears, cries and frowns. For me that luggage represented fear. I allowed fear to prevent me from dealing with all the things that everyday life is comprised of.

Due to the hurt and heartache that I experienced when my brother took his life, I knew that I had to address the fears that had become a part of my existence. Becoming a better me was no longer an option it was now a requirement. I had to look at the person in the mirror and make the necessary changes for me to become a better me. I didn't like looking in the mirror because nothing can be hidden when you look in the mirror, you see yourself as you really are. Yes, I wanted to become a better me, not just for me, but for my son. He deserves the best that I can give him and that is exactly what he is going to get.

It was never my place to judge my parents on their Parenting Skills or the lack of, but I do have a responsibility to make better choices that will allow me as a parent to equip my son with the tools that he will need on his journey in life. We did not have a choice in the parents that we have but there was a purpose behind it. You see when situations seem to go from bad to worse, there is still something good in that situation. More times than not individuals that had those difficult situations chose to use those situations as stairs to climb in life.

I have decided that I can no longer mope around or feel sad inside because of the choice that my brother made. I am not nor will I be responsible for the action that he chose. Needless to say if I chose to carry that burden it would definitely be in vain. He is my brother that is no longer among the living and he is resting in his grave and God has his spirit.

Now that it has been said and done, I know that I still have things that I need to clean out of my mental closet. I see the Dark Storm Cloud beginning to drift away, as I look up, I can see the sun peeking through. Before the sun shines bright, I have to look at the **Pieces of Me**.

CPSIA information can be obtained at www.ICGtesting.com
Printed in the USA
LVOW08s1011181013

357427LV00001B/90/P

9 781490 715285